Pigeons in the Subway

Emilee, Eira, Muthu, and Vlada
Art by Rachael Smith

Emmemm Publishing • New York • Mercer Island

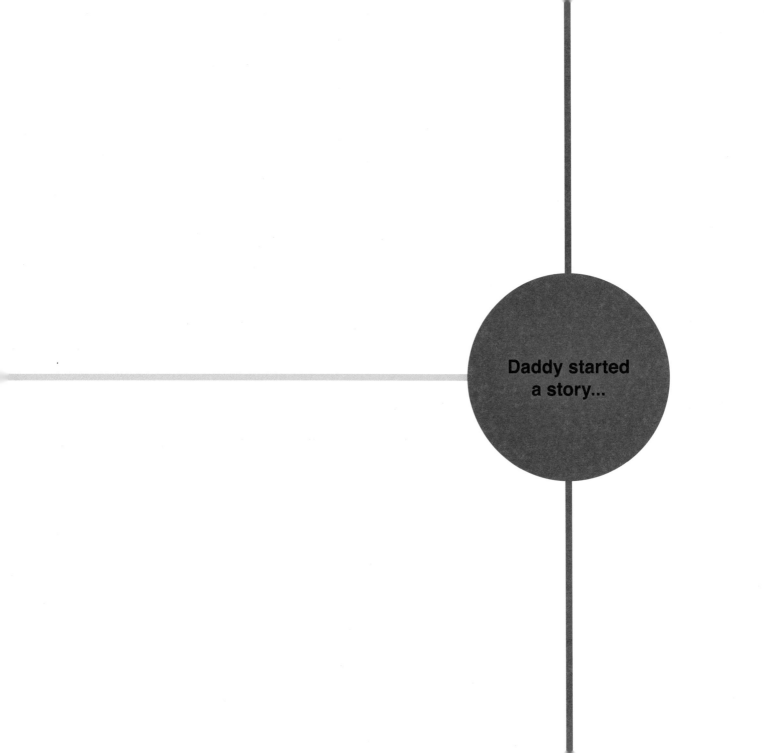

Daddy started
a story...

It was bedtime.

The girls
Eira and Emilee
crowded onto
one bed.

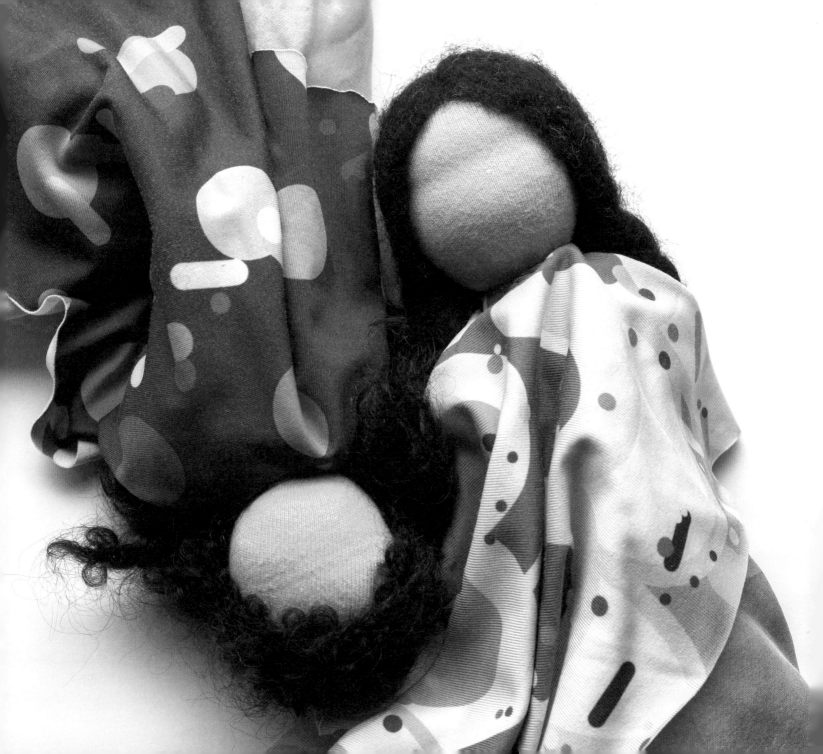

They had
two girl
pigeons

and two boy
pigeons.

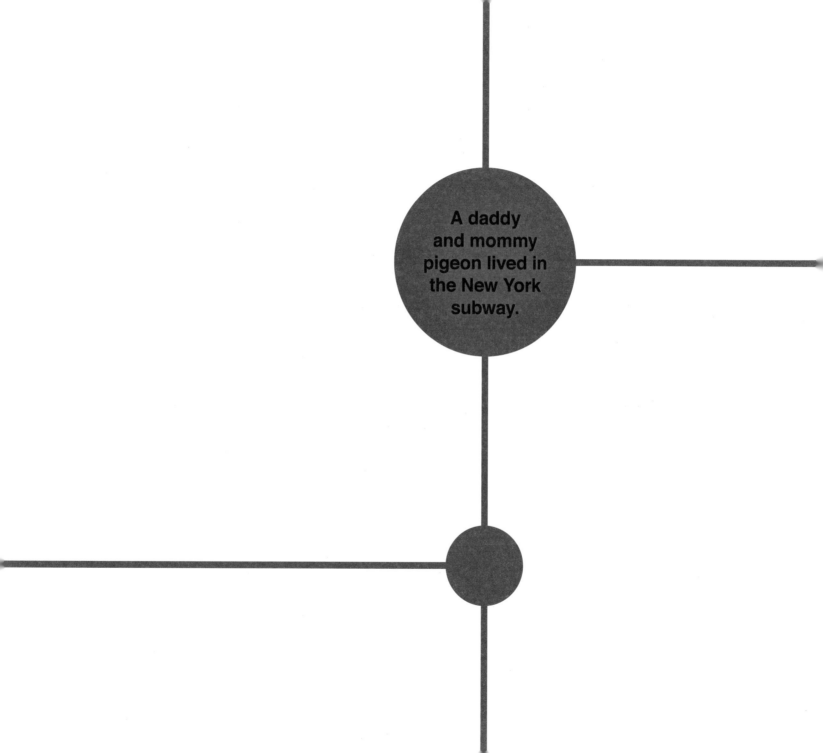

A daddy
and mommy
pigeon lived in
the New York
subway.

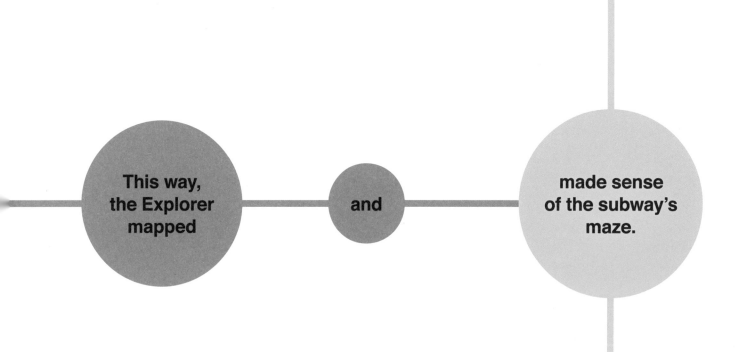

This way, the Explorer mapped and made sense of the subway's maze.

The older girl pigeon was an explorer.

She crawled through crevices,
pursued veering tracks,
and flapped through abandoned stations.

their pets,
and their heeled strides.

This way,
the Observer
tracked
trends

and
made sense
of the
seasons

beyond
the subway.

The little girl pigeon was an observer.

She noticed people: lines on their faces, textures of their bags, colors of their hats,

This way
the Counter
clicked
through events,

and figured out the patterns
from mornings to after-hours.

created
mathematical
memories,

and made
sense
of the subway's
statistical
rhythms.

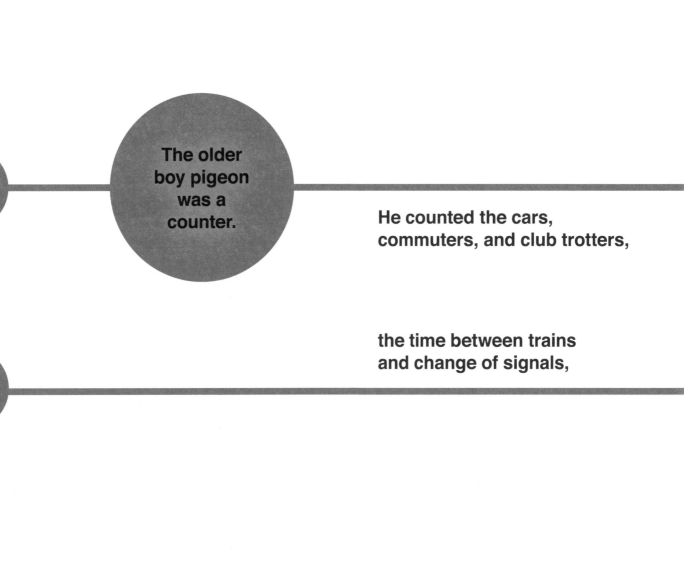

The older boy pigeon was a counter.

He counted the cars, commuters, and club trotters,

the time between trains and change of signals,

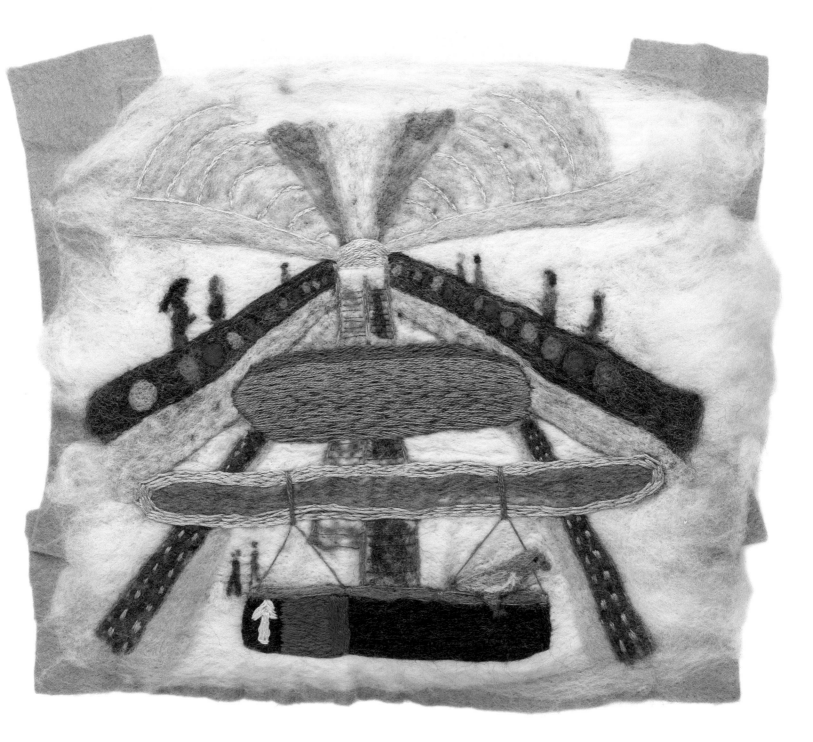

This way
the Gatherer
collected
edibles

and

poppy seed bagels with whitefish salad,
sodas, smart water, and abandoned coffee.

made sense
of the source of
all life
in the subway.

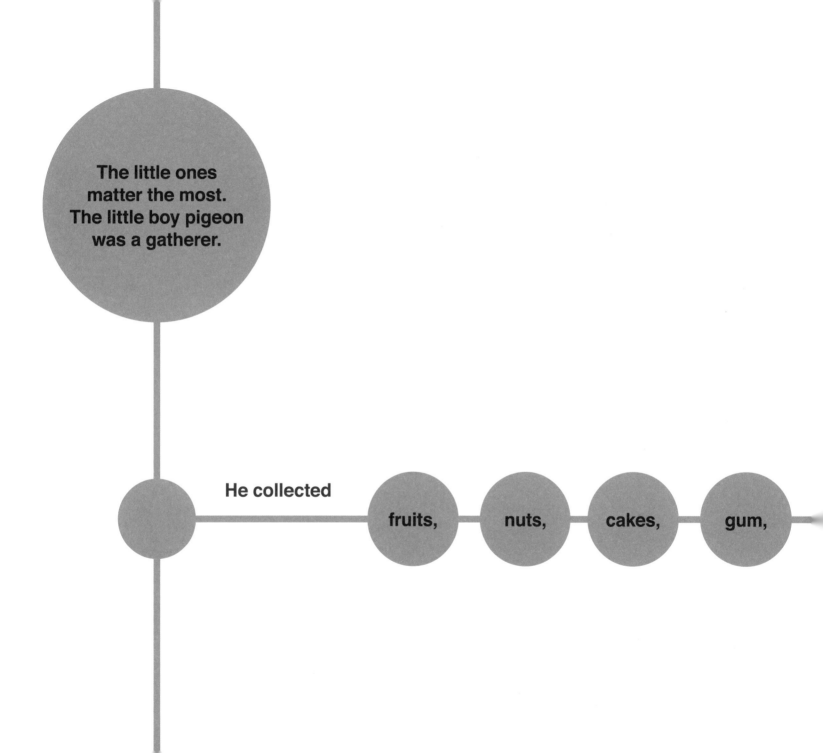

The little ones matter the most. The little boy pigeon was a gatherer.

He collected

fruits,

nuts,

cakes,

gum,

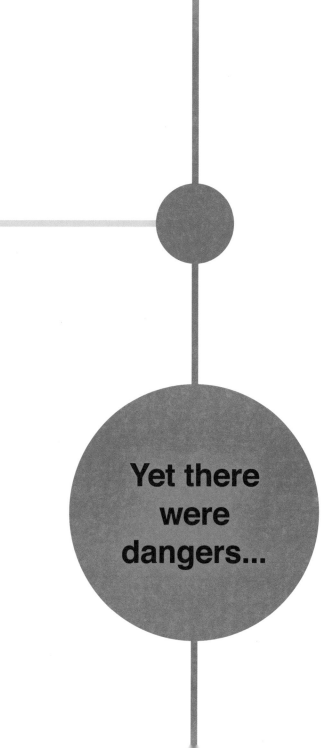

Yet there
were
dangers...

The pigeon family lived and learned in the subway.

No one shooed them away.

A loud voice said,

"Stand clear of the closing doors, please!"

Immediately the door shut behind her.

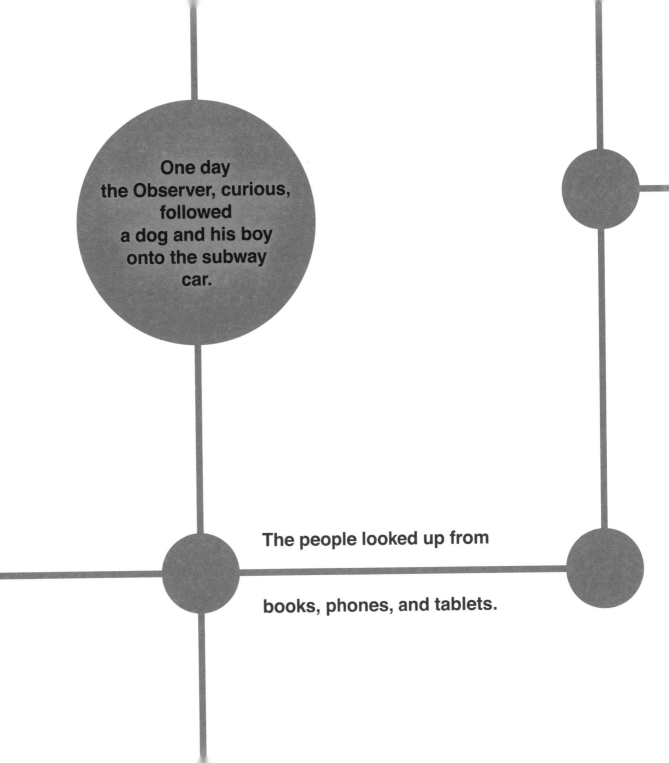

One day
the Observer, curious,
followed
a dog and his boy
onto the subway
car.

The people looked up from

books, phones, and tablets.

ed flaps,
d in the wake of the speeding train
gent shadow.

The father pigeon
raised his beak in defense
and spread his wings.
The little pigeons
gathered underneath.

The Counter
grunted
in alarm
and
turned to Mom.

But the mother pigeon
had already seen
the debacle
and started flying
behind the train.

With de
she f
lik

So the children squeezed
in on the father's back,

who puffed and powered
through the labyrinth,

following the train
they could now only hear.

The father pigeon
knew
families
belonged together.

The Counter calculated and figured they had time
to get to a stop before the next train chased them
down the tunnel.

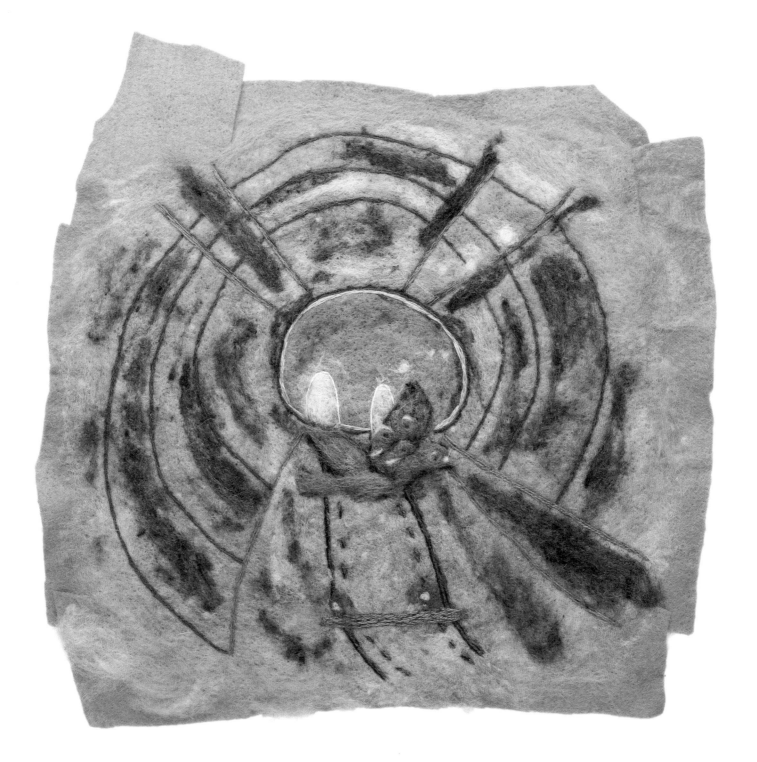

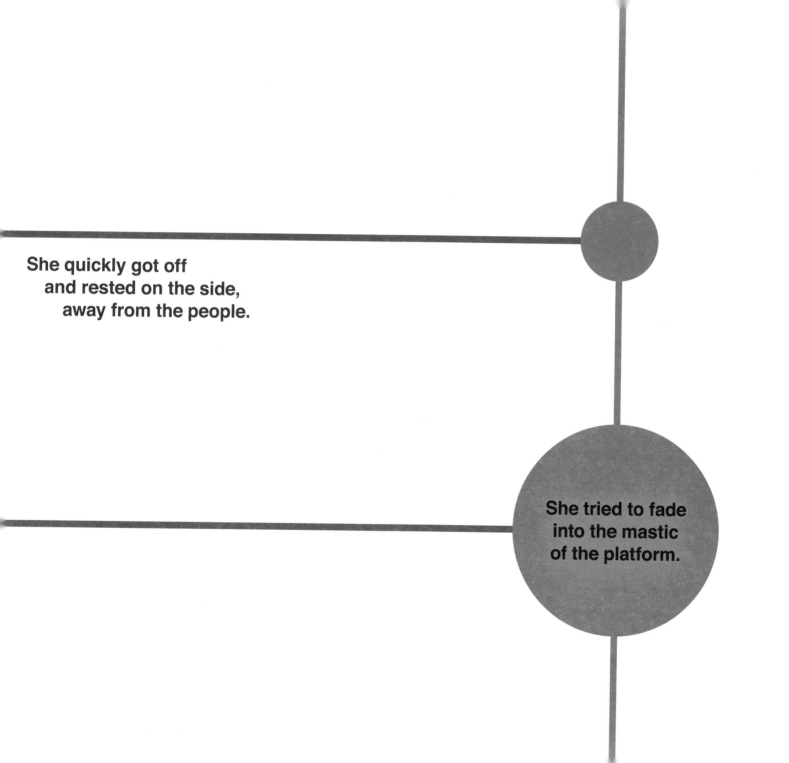

She quickly got off
and rested on the side,
away from the people.

She tried to fade
into the mastic
of the platform.

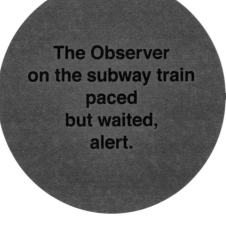

The Observer on the subway train paced but waited, alert.

The train swayed, slowed, and came to a stop.

She found
the Observer

and landed
by her side.

Shortly after,
the mother pigeon
arrived.

Breathless,
she searched
the length of the platform.

They found the heaving mother next to the contrite Observer and landed next to them.

The End.

Soon after,
the father pigeon
also arrived,
breathing hard,
with two pigeons
on his back.

The Explorer had jumped out ahead
to lead them through shortcuts that she knew well.

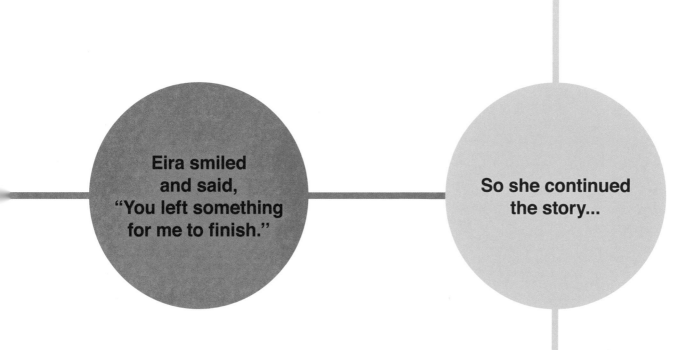

Eira smiled and said, "You left something for me to finish."

So she continued the story...

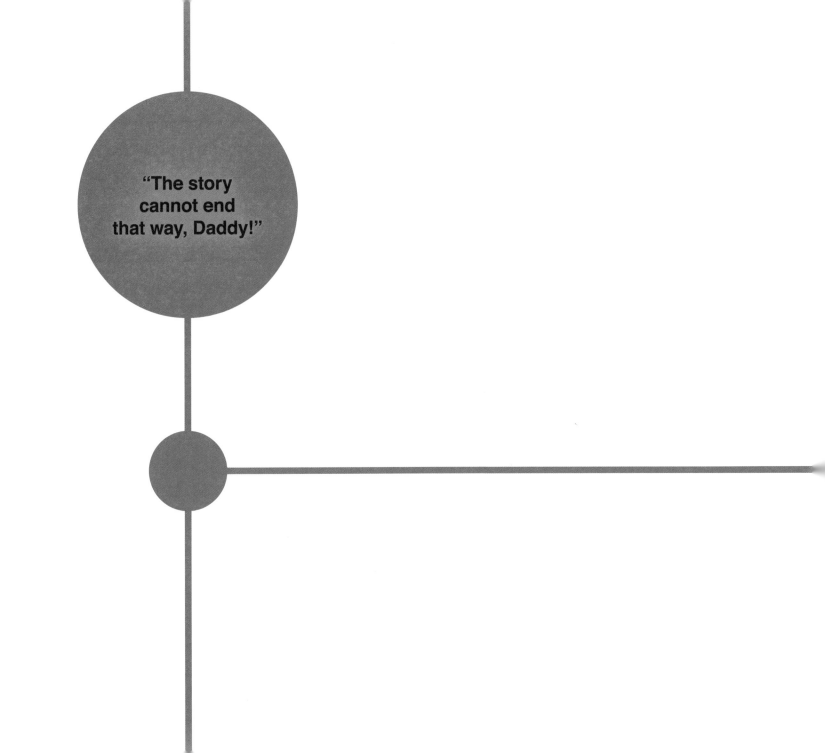

"The story
cannot end
that way, Daddy!"

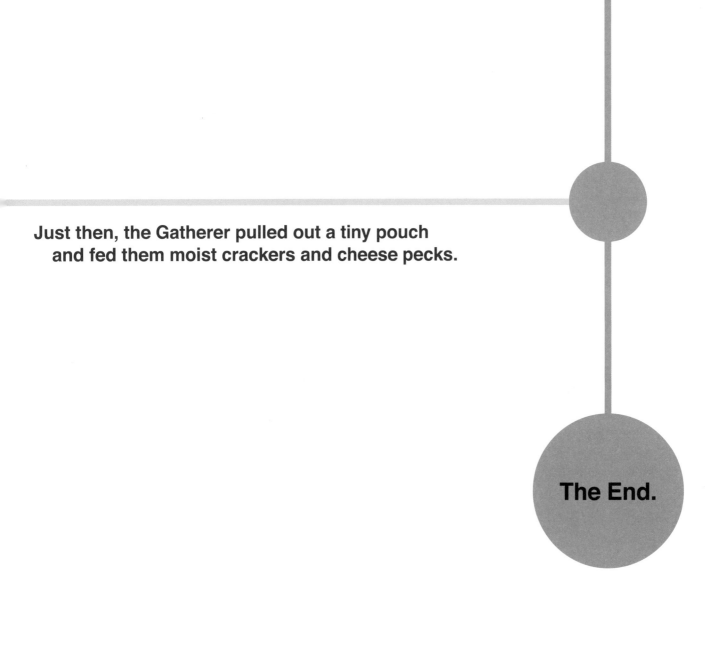

Just then, the Gatherer pulled out a tiny pouch
   and fed them moist crackers and cheese pecks.

The End.

The family huddled close, tired.

"Families find a way,"
Eira soothed.

"Always,"
Daddy added.

Time to sleep!"
Mommy
chimed in.

"There will be other
dangers,
Daddy, Mommy,"
Emilee said.

Daddy answered,

"There is a bit in each of you
of the Observer, Explorer,
Counter and Gatherer,
in no particular order.

Sometimes you are one,
sometimes one of the others.

Stories are made to be
a fabric of all of us."

But the girls went to bed,
each believing
they were really one
or the other.

Emilee asked,

"Was the Observer me, Daddy?
Like the Observer,
I watch things and do art with
shapes and textures."

Eira asked,

"Was the Explorer me, Daddy?
Like the Explorer,
I like climbing, running fast,
and hunting for treasures."

Other books from Emmemm Publishing

Sunday with Dad

Eira documents a seemingly ordinary day with her dad and her little sister. It is not ordinary to Eira though; it is a day of doing and learning new things, no mewling.

A Squirrel Thrives

A little squirrel does push-ups and learns to climb a tree. But once you learn something, there is always the next thing to learn.

Unicorns in Gymnastica

In Gymnastica all animals are unicorns, using their horns to hunt, play, and paint. Authors create this fantastic world and reminisce about stuffies and humans in Gymnastica.

The Redwood Tree and Its Friends

Eira and her dad explore friendships between a growing redwood tree and other creatures. The redwood learns from its friends but outgrows them. Eira finds a way to bring the friendships back.

Left and Right

Eira and her dad explore the dialogue between the left and right parts of one's body during their outdoor play. When they reach the lonely heart, Eira finds a way to bring all the parts together.

Todler of Arts: Year 2

Emilee created these artworks as a two-year-old toddler at her school. Each artwork here appears with Emilee's caption and a background note related to the caption provided by her family.

What can readers do?

Readers can be writers, artists, and doers.

Be writers:
Change the pigeons' personalities and invent other dangers the family overcomes.

Be artists:
Create your own felt scenes and embroidered characters.

Be doers:
Collaborate on your own family adventures and overcome challenges.

Artist

Rachael Smith teaches at a Waldorf-inspired School in Fallbrook, California. She has lived in many locations across the world, including Edinburgh, London, Singapore, and Hong Kong, and loves to go on summerlong trips to far off destinations. She finds inspiration in travel and nature, and feels equally at home in a backyard garden or bustling city. Her joy for storytelling, handiwork, and teaching animates her personal life as well as her work as a teacher and artist.

Art

The artist worked with wool, felt, silk, and cotton thread to produce the art for this book. The silk marionettes are in the style of Waldorf puppets. The subway and pigeon images are made on felt and combine the techniques of needle felting and embroidery. Whereas the needle felting seeks to express the sweep and character of the pigeons and the people amid a specific range of colors, the embroidery highlights the textural details, such as the tiles and edges of the subways stations. Each piece serves as an invitation into the gentle and whimsical world of the story.

Collaboration

A family of mourning doves nested outside the kids' bedroom in Tribeca, and it triggered Dad's story about pigeons in urbanscapes. The family quickly chimed in and created the personalities. The pigeon caught in the subway was inspired by an article about pigeons sharing the subway with commuters. The family supplied the rest of the story, including the dialogue. It was a collaborative family story that lived on in our discussions for several months. Later when Eira's school did a project on birds, one of her exercises asked, "Where do pigeons live?" and she responded, "In the subway."

Rachael settled on a combination of felt, embroidery, and marionettes for the artwork and incorporated fabric into the work since texture is pivotal to the story of the Observer pigeon. Eira and Emilee collaborated with Rachael by taking her to subway stations in New York and helped work out the motifs. Rachael keenly developed the personalities of the pigeons. When she worked on the art, her nephews and nieces chipped in with suggestions, making this a collaborative project across families.